What Happened

A Care and Sc⸺ ⸺a

By

D. A. Knight

ACKNOWLEDGEMENTS

With thanks to Steve and Lucy, Sue Knight for editing, Caspar Graham for the cover design. Jo, Sandra, Colette, Mum and Helen for being my first readers. Dad, Sarah and Isabel for their valued support.

To Steve and Lucy

ONE

I walked into the room and every face turned my way. I'd like to say that this happens often, that I am a stunning six foot blonde but that would be a lie.

My name is Phyllis Care pronounced Car – ay. My name should have an accent but my editor says they are too distracting and expensive. No one ever forgets his apostrophe though.

"Care where are you?"

"Coming Mr De'Ath ." (See what I mean.)

"Have you got me the golf club story yet Care?" he boomed.

I'm a junior reporter on the Dibbington News and I'd been sent to the golf club to investigate reports of financial anomalies. So, as I was saying, I walked into the Dibbington Golf Club bar and everyone froze.

Oswin Smarmer, the pro, had been regaling Felicity Thorp with his tale of a hole in one back in 2002. How could I tell? Her mouth was so far open in a monstrous yawn that the entire room could see her tonsils. Reggie Parsons was hopping from one foot to the other looking as if he was having difficulty holding something in. Turns out he needed the loo, he pushed past me apologising and I swear I saw seepage around the pantular area. It was not pleasant.

Just as conversation resumed a scream rent the air and Reggie, trousers at half-mast ran, into the room pointing and trying to say something.

Being a reporter I naturally sprang into action and followed the direction of the pointing to the men's bathroom. At first glance nothing seemed amiss. The smells, although unfamiliar, seemed very toilet like but on closer inspection the doors to the cubicles were all slightly ajar and one grabbed my interest as there was a foot sticking out. It was unnaturally still and at an odd angle.

I had to tell my feet quite firmly to move in the direction of that unmoving foot and then command my eyes to take in the sight before them. There was a man sitting on the toilet in a state of dishabille. I understand from my colleagues, in obituaries, that it is more common to be found dead on a toilet than one would suppose. I for one have never before thought about the indignity involved but this sight forced me to.

Thankfully a copy of our illustrious paper covered the man's privates, just, and my bashful nature (yes I know this seems unlikely for a journalist but even I have my limits) precluded me investigating further. I was just about to exit the cubicle when the corpse gave an almighty snore and I yelped, jumped and hit my head on the door frame as I tried to make a sharp egress.

Clutching my head I turned round to find Oswin Smarmer immediately behind me and much closer than I would like.

"Can I help you Babe?" he said from inside my personal space.

"Perhaps you could see if there's a doctor on the premises," I said smiling in what I hoped was a flirty way. He grimaced slightly and nodded. Note to self, work on flirting techniques.

I pushed the door of the cubicle to slightly and waited. Then I had a thought that Mr De'Ath wouldn't like to see the paper used in this way so put my hand round the door, pulled the paper from the man's hands and shoved it into my copious bag.

TWO

"Care! Care! What the heck is this envelope doing on my desk? Is it anything to do with you?"

I rushed into the office mid article. "No Mr De'Ath. Never seen it before."

He gingerly pried his finger under the sticky brown flap, pulled out a photograph and turned a funny green colour dropping it onto the desk. "Is this some kind of joke? I ought to fire you for this Care."

I picked up the photo. It was of the man at the golf club, still holding the newspaper that I had carefully removed before anyone else had seen it; underneath it read 'Golfer found asleep on toilet after reading the Dibbington News. Editor Charles De'Ath has no comment to make.'

"Well! Do you have something to say Care?"

"I told you I removed the paper before anyone could see it," I said.

"And......"

"And clearly I was not the first person on the scene Mr De'Ath,"

"You think Care…….mmmmm………..you think!" he said waving the photo at me.

"I'll just get back to finishing my article. Perhaps it will be the last we hear of it." I didn't believe it and neither did Mr De'Ath but what could I do? My mind kept returning to the scene of the incident. What had I missed?

To conclude my article I named the golfer on the toilet as Brian Weatherall, an amateur golfer/tennis pro who, it appeared, had had one too many whiskeys at the club bar. I didn't mention the newspaper and hoped that the photograph would not find its way to one of our rival papers.

It was a vain hope. The next day the Dibbington Times led on the picture with the headline.

'The "News" too boring for Golfers'

Mr De'Ath was incandescent. I decided to take a trip out of the office to hunt for stories. My search led me back to the golf club. I know I'm a glutton for punishment but what else was I to do? My head told me there was more to be had from this story even though my instinct was to remain as far away from the place as possible. My head won.

I entered the bar; déjà vu. The same people turned and looked at me but returned to their normal conversation even sooner than yesterday. That's what I was yesterday's news. Only a few titters from the corner, where Oswin Smarmer was entertaining a lady of indeterminate years, told the story of my humiliating experience at the hands of the Dibbington Times.

It wasn't long before my personal space invader made his way over.

"Miss Care how lovely to see you. I hope we're not keeping you up?" Oswin smiled at his own joke and I bit my tongue to prevent myself from the retort that sprang to my lips.

"Thank you Mr Smarmer I'm quite awake. How are things today? Any further titbits to pass my way? I'm always up for a story," I said smiling to hide my inner sickness at my proximity to the oily slickness oozing before me.

"Well I did hear that the Major was pining for Felicity's company. Apparently she didn't show up this morning for their usual tete a tete. He was beginning to think he had lost his charm but I'm sure that can't be it. Felicity's been hanging off his every word since his recent lottery win," Oswin said, hiding his mouth with his hand as if that would prevent his voice from carrying to every corner of the room.

I too had seen the way Felicity looked, at the Major's wallet, such loyalty would be hard to fake. I decided to call on Felicity Thorp at the earliest opportunity.

THREE

No one home; back door; no answer.

What to do now? I couldn't legally enter the building and without Felicity I had no story. I turned back to the car and just as I was about to drive off the Major himself drove up in his beige Bentley. I ducked. He looked left and right and when he saw no one was about he walked towards the front door. He had a key.

I left it five minutes and then knocked on the front door again.

The net curtain behind the front bay window twitched.

I knocked again, this time shouting,

"Major! I know you're in there. I need to speak with Felicity," I said.

"Well you can't. She's indisposed."

"What do you mean she's indisposed? Is she naked or something?" I said.

"No. It's just...... go away," he shouted.

"I'm not going anywhere," I said as I sat in the front door step.

I was prepared to sit for as long as it took. Well at least as long as it took the coffee I'd just drunk to work its way through my system. I wasn't really one of those self-sacrificing reporters which was probably why I was still working at the Dibbington News.

"You can't just sit there," the Major shouted, "people will talk."

"They'll talk even more if you keep shouting at me," I said and began singing Row Row Row your Boat very loudly in an off key Alto. What I lacked in pitch I made up for in volume. The net curtains were now twitching all down the street.

"Alright Alright but you must promise not to take any pictures or report on this in any way," the Major said.

"I promise," I said with my fingers firmly crossed behind my back.

The door opened and the Major ushered me into the house. Nothing out of the ordinary in the front room. He led me upstairs to the bedroom where Felicity lay ominously still on the bed. Across her face like a child's make believe tent was a copy of the Dibbington News.

"Is she.....you know?" I said.

"What? No……..no. She's alive but she appears to be drugged or something I can't seem to wake her. I tried shaking her. I was just going to get some cold water when you started hollering at the front door."

"I wasn't hollering. That was singing."

"I didn't mean the singing," the Major said, "although that was quite bad."

"What were you saying about not reporting this?" I said folding my arms.

Felicity let out a moan.

"Felicity darling. It's me Bertie wertie."

(Bertie wertie!)

Another moan.

"Shall I call an ambulance?" I said.

Anything to get me out of this overly pink and perfumed boudoir and from any further Bertie werties or Felicity wicity. Make me want to barf.

"Yes probably," the Major said.

"Sorry probably what," I said lost in the icky fantasy.

"Ambulance," he said.

"Right; ambulance."

By the time the paramedics arrived Felicity was fully awake and we were starting to feel foolish for calling them out. However the first paramedic took one look in Felicity's eyes and insisted she go to the hospital.

The paper was now lying on the floor.

I surreptitiously scooped it into my bag and this time, with the exception of the Major, I was sure that I had been the first on the scene.

FOUR

"This is becoming a habit. What is it with you Care? You want us to lose readers." Mr De'Ath was on the war path.

"Well to be fair sir the readership has actually increased since the two recent incidents so…" I started to say.

"That's because we're a laughing stock Care. You said you were first on the scene. What happened this time?"

I had thought and thought but come up with very little. I had been outside the house just before the Major arrived and there had been no one else there.

"I don't know. I'll go and talk with Felicity now she's out of hospital see if she has a clue," I said.

I also wanted to talk to her about what the paramedics had been worried about, it might help me find the culprit.

The police laughed in Mr De'Ath's face when he had suggested that the photographs and captions may be a form of blackmail.

He had almost exploded when the second photograph had arrived in the post the morning after we had run the story with the caption, "The Dibbington News even too boring for the Major's girlfriend." He had binned it before the Major caught wind of it but it seemed the Major had received the same photograph in the post and was not in the least amused blaming Mr De'Ath for it all despite their years of friendship.

"It won't do you hear me? First you send that pesky girl round to my beloved's house and now it turns out it's someone with a grudge against you. I want it sorted!" he slammed the phone down. It was after this call that I had been hauled into his office.

Felicity was at home and answered the door looking none the worse for her ordeal.

"Well after all it was only a bit of extra sleep and who could complain about that?" she said indicating I should sit down on her puffy purple sofa.

"Do you have any idea what happened?" I asked.

"No I'd got up as usual. Made myself some tea and went back upstairs to read the paper. Next thing I know Albert was there and you were on the phone talking loudly."

"Yeah sorry about that. Nothing else, no one watching the house or following you when you were out and about?"

"Not that I noticed. No." Felicity said, shifting in her seat.

"By the way what paper do you read?" I said as an afterthought.

"The Times why?" Felicity said.

"No reason. Thanks for your help," I said and got up to leave.

"Actually Miss Care there was something odd when I got back yesterday. My teapot was washed and put away. You didn't happen to do it before you left did you?" Felicity said.

I nearly snorted with laughter as I shook my head.

"What about the Major?" I said.

It was her turn to laugh with a more delicate snort than my own.

"The Major prides himself on the fact that he has never raised a hand in the kitchen in his life," Felicity said.

"Well. Good luck with that then," I said.

"What do you mean? I think you'd better leave if you are going to insult my Bertie Wertie," Felicity said firmly shutting the door behind me.

So much for tact and diplomacy.

Now for the paramedic.

FIVE

"You know I can't tell you that. I'll be sacked," Keith said when I caught him having a quick doughnut at the back of the hospital. He waved the doughnut in my general direction.

"S'posed to have given them up. My wife's got me on a diet!"

Seeing a weakness I pounced.

"You live next door to my Auntie Sue don't you?" I said.

"No," Keith said unconvincingly.

"I know your wife. She's the head of the local gardening association isn't she?"

"No," Keith said again looking more and more worried.

"I'm going to tea at Sue's tomorrow afternoon. Think I'll pop round and say hi," I said placing my pen and pad into my back pocket and making as if to walk away.

"Wait alright I'll tell you."

That was easy.

"I'm listening," I said pen poised.

"She was drugged. They think someone put something in her tea but I didn't tell you and I will deny ever having this conversation okay?" he said and fairly sprinted back into the hospital.

"Drugged?"

Drugged.

That explained a few things. Perhaps the person who drugged her had plenty of time to take the photograph and then scarper before I appeared on the scene.

What about the man on the golf club toilet? Had he too been drugged? Had he even been tested?

I decided to call in a favour. I'd known Detective Inspector Scott since I had rescued him from bullies when I was a prefect at school and he was in Year eight. The incident had not only caused a slightly embarrassing case of hero worship on his part (who am I kidding I loved it!) but had instilled in him a sense of justice and community spirit that led to his current position with the local constabulary. I, of course, approached the subject with my usual diplomacy and tact.

"Here Scott what's this I hear about Felicity Thorp being drugged?" I said as he exited the –shire police station.

For my reward he grabbed my upper arm and practically dragged me into an interrogation room. I'd forgotten how gorgeous he was; I must not weaken.

"How much of this are you going to report?" he said.

"Depends," I said,

"On what?"

"On what you tell me," I said leaning forward.

"Well suppose I tell you nothing?" Reece Scott said leaning closer to me.

We were a little too close for comfort and definitely too close for me to think straight. I pulled back and he smiled lazily.

"What if I ask some questions and you nod in the right places?" I said as a compromise.

"That might work. Go ahead. I can't stop you asking questions?" he said sinking back in his chair.

The distance between us kicked my brain back into gear.

"Was Felicity drugged?" I asked.

A nod.

"Was it her tea?"

A shrug.

"Did you see the photograph someone sent the Major?" I said.

A wide smile.

"Is there any other link to the man found in the gents at the golf club?"

Another shrug.

"Was he drugged too?" I said.

A frown.

"You mean you hadn't thought to investigate that?" I said.

"No, of course we're investigating it but it just occurred to me that the link might be sitting right in front of me," Reece Scott said leaning forward again.

"Okay well thanks for your help got to go. Take care. See you around," I said rising hurriedly and backing towards the door.

He was too quick for me and leaned over looking directly into my eyes. I found it even more difficult to concentrate with him this close and stood mutely hoping that he didn't really mean to carry out the threat implicit in his eyes.

"You might not want to hide anything from me," he said, "I owe you but I'm not about to lose my job over you."

"Okay. I'll tell you anything I know; honest."

"An honest reporter. That'll be the day," he said, "off you go; for now."

He called out after me.

"Don't do anything to make me arrest you Care?"

SIX

As if!

I mean, I'd never done anything actually illegal before. Like the door of the house belonging to the guy at the golf club was definitely open when I went through it. I was only wearing gloves when I had a quick look through his draws because I didn't want to confuse the police case. Nothing there; just a few receipts from the local café and a bottle of nail polish in the slightly dubious shade of Passionate Peony. I hadn't really studied the guys finger nails when he had been sitting on the toilet so couldn't be sure that it wasn't his.

My phone rang with a well-known shark film theme – De'Ath.

Better answer it.

"Mr De'Ath how can I help you?" I spoke quickly and held the phone away from my ear so as not to be deafened by his instant bellowing. It went on for about a minute and then absolute silence. I tentatively put the phone back to my ear.

"Gotcha! Now listen to me Care, get over to the golf club. He's struck again but this time he e-mailed me a photo first and said "Come and get me!" Bloody cheek! Get over there quick. He's behind the ninth, if my memory serves me correctly. Move it!"

"Yes sir," I said to thin air.

The amount of time Sir spent at the golf club I would trust him to have the location right but it was still very little to go on. I approached the ninth hole with some trepidation when a ball whizzed over my head at the same time as a loud voice behind me shouted,

"Fore!"

The Major appeared from the rough and waved a greeting to me with his nine iron.

"Morning Miss. You looking out for sleeping golfers what eh?" the Major said walking in my direction.

I laughed in what I hoped was a casual manner. "No, no just out for a morning stroll. You know how it is. How's Mrs Thorp?"

"Fine fine. Staying at mine for the moment. Scared of going home. Done me a favour that pervert has," he said and gave me a lascivious wink.

"Okay Major. I'll see you later," I said and moved off further into the rough and a patch of woodland behind it that looked promising for hiding a sleeping person of indeterminate size.

After about five minutes I was cursing the fact that it was a warm day and I had chosen to wear shorts. My legs were a tangle of red scratches and I was no closer to finding our victim. Perhaps the whole thing had been a hoax. Perhaps it had been a diversion. There was no sign of anyone having been through these woods before me for some time and surely dragging a sleeping body would have left some mark. Maybe Mr D. was off in his identification of the area involved. I retraced my steps and made my way over to the club house. In the bar a lady was weeping into her drink and Oswin Smarmer was taking what, I can only describe, as full advantage of the situation. He was draped over her shoulders one eye on her cleavage and the other on her Rolex.

"Oh, Oswin you are so kind," she managed between sobs. "It was so frightening. One minute I was taking tea on the terrace the next I woke up on the green propped up by the flag with this rag of a newspaper on my head. I feel so humiliated. I mean I would never be caught dead reading such trash."

I was beginning to feel much less sorry for her. However I am a reporter and I needed the story. "I've just heard," I said all sympathy, "can I help?"

"Who are you?" she said looking at me as if I was a particularly nasty bug she wished to tread on.

"I'm a reporter for the ………Times," I said improvising.

Oswin Smarmer looked at me with a fierce expression but then shrugged and turned his attention back to cleavage lady.

"Oh it was awful. Let me tell you all about it," she said.

SEVEN

An hour later my ears ringing with the sound of clipped vowels I left the bar having persuaded the lady, Donna, to report the matter to Detective Inspector Reece Scott as soon as possible.

It was all very strange. Nothing had been stolen despite her having an eye watering amount of cash in her purse. Apart from a slight headache she felt fine and was obviously enjoying Oswin's overt attentions.

I slunk back to the office to be confronted with the photo on my desk and a note in bold letters – UNLESS YOU SORT THIS OUT THIS WEEK CARE YOU ARE FIRED!!! I looked over at Sir's office but he was out.

Phew!

I looked through my notes trying to find a clue, anything that might lead me to the person behind this. It wasn't just job preservation either, what Reece had said earlier started to hit home. The only link that I could find between these people was the golf club and me. I did not find my conclusions comfortable. I was always the first or one of the first people on the scene. If I was the police I would suspect me too.

I knew a little about the second victim but not very much about the first and third. I'd try Donna later when she had escaped the clutches of Mr Smarmer.

First Brian.

Sources told me that he could be found either at the golf club or the tennis club. I'd not spotted him this morning so I tried the latter.

Brian, now in full possession of his trousers, was a man in his mid- fifties with pepper and salt grey hair and a paunch. He may have once been handsome but had gone to seed. His tennis playing seemed to consist mainly of catching up on his tan and returning the ball over the net from a machine seemingly set at snail pace. It barely warranted a flick of his wrist but several females on the side lines were shrieking at every effort as if he had just won Wimbledon.

I tried joining them and their screaming in a bid to ingratiate myself with him but really couldn't stomach it. I decided to tackle him on his next drinks break. He had been unconscious the last time I saw him and hopefully my picture in the paper was airbrushed enough that he wouldn't recognise me. The screaming mercifully abated and I made my move.

"Mr Weatherall?" I said smiling in what I hoped was an inane and devoted looking way.

"Yes my dear?"

(Oh dear!)

I fluttered my eyelashes in what I hoped was an alluring way but he stepped backwards sharply.

"Do you have something in your eye my dear?" he asked politely.

"Oh er, yes. A fly", I said blinking furiously.

"Can I help?" he said pulling out a monogrammed handkerchief.

"No I think it's gone. Yes, yes it has."

"That's good. Well must be going," Brian said.

"Did I see you in the paper the other day?" I said.

He coloured up and began looking about for a route of escape. "Yes you might have done. Bit embarrassing that," Brian said.

"Not at all. I couldn't help thinking what a fine figure of a man you looked," I said with a perfectly straight face.

"Why thank you my dear. That's very kind of you," Brian said pulling in his stomach and puffing out his chest.

I had never seen anyone actually do that before a bit like a peacock.

"How on earth did that happen? I mean did you feel unwell? It must have been quite horrible," I said.

"Yes it was. How kind you are. Yes as a matter of fact I did feel unwell which was why I went into the gents in the first place," Brian said, "I'm sorry to mention the gentleman's room in front of you my dear."

(Really!)

"Actually now that I think about it I had begun to feel tired as I left home that morning but had been fighting it until, unfortunately, as you saw..........."

"Thank you Mr Weatherall for taking the time to talk with me," I said, "perhaps you should mention the tiredness to the police".

"Yes I will. What an astute young lady you are Miss Care."

EIGHT

It was the second time in two days that a man had seen right through me. I needed a certain degree of mystery in my job. I was failing miserably. If I didn't improve soon I would be fired and what else would I do, I wasn't qualified for anything. I didn't want to do anything else. Why couldn't I get a break on this story?

Oh great, here comes P C Handsome, (I think he's handsome?)

"Hello Reece. Come to arrest me?" I said in what I hoped was a light tone.

"Not yet Care but I will if you keep tampering with my witnesses," he said fixing me with a bearlike stare.

"I rise with every attempt to intimidate me," I said, gaily misquoting Elizabeth Bennett.

"It isn't my intention to intimidate Care. Interfering with a witness is an offence you know. It's my job to enforce the law."

"I did tell them to tell you what they told me," I said.

"So you did and I suppose you want thanks for that," Reece said.

"No. Just the odd exchange of information now and then," I said, pushing my luck.

"For instance?"

"Well Donna for instance. Same M.O. as the others?"

The briefest of nods.

"Are we thinking it's the same person?" I said.

He moved closer. "Aha," he said.

"Any idea who?" I said.

"Mmm" he said invading my personal space in a most personal way.

"Who?" I said in barely more than a squeak.

"I think that it's a nosey reporter, who fed up with not having anything to write about, has decided to make up her own story so that she can grab an exclusive and sell it to the nationals for a fortune."

"Really?" I said my voice now so high pitched that even a dog would have difficulty hearing it.

"Really," he said.

His face was centimetres from mine.

"It's a good job that I know this particular reporter and that she's basically too law abiding to do anything of the sort. Isn't that right?"

I couldn't speak.

He pulled back.

"See you around Care," he said and walked off.

That's it. He just turns me to mush and then walks away. I will not let this happen again. I will not be anyone's puppet. How dare he? I am a strong independent woman.

My mobile rang.

"Care get back to the office someone called Donna wants to see you. She's waiting in my office and is demanding coffee and biscuits. Hurry up!"

"Yes sir immediately," I said.

See; strong, independent.

I could hear Donna issuing orders as soon as I exited the lift.

"No. I said two sugars. Can nobody round here get anything right?"

I put my handbag on my desk and picked up a pen. I would not be rushed.

"You, reporter girl. I saw you at the golf club where that delectable Oswin was being so helpful. You wanted to speak to me. Well here I am. Make it quick I'm very busy," Donna said staring intently at her manicure.

"Mrs er?" I said looking through my notes.

"Miss Smart," she said.

"Miss Smart. Did you notice anything unusual about your morning before…?"

I said searching for the politest words I could think of.

"Before I found myself asleep on the ninth green, propped against a flag pole with your beastly paper over my face?" Donna said.

"Well, yes," I said pen poised.

"Nothing really. I'd just been having breakfast in the club house. Wandered out to watch something Oswin was doing and next thing I know I woke up where he found me," she said.

"Did Oswin see anything?" I said.

"Well you'll have to ask him that won't you?" she said testily.

"One more thing. What did you eat for breakfast?"

"Poached egg on wholemeal toast and tea. Same as usual."

"Thank you Miss Smart. You've been very helpful," I said.

"I have?" she said.

"You have," I said.

"Oh!"

NINE

"Why'd you tell her she'd been helpful?" Mr De'Ath said as I relayed the interview to him.

"My mother taught me to always be polite," I said, "anyway she's told us more than she knows."

"Care to enlighten me Care?"

"Not yet Sir, just need to think for a while and go and see Oswin Smarmer."

"Better change into trousers then Care."

Looking down at my rather conservative length skirt. I thought why should I? Then I remembered Oswin Smarmer's wandering hands and took his point. A home visit and a wardrobe ransacking later I arrived at the golf club in my only pair of tailored black trousers.

Oswin was on his usual stool at the bar. It amazed me how he managed to keep his figure but perhaps he spent all of his non-bar time at the gym. He greeted me like an old friend and answered my questions with barely concealed enthusiasm.

"Well as it happens I do remember Donna standing on the veranda. One likes to keep abreast of what the ladies are up to, you know. Good for business. Anyway, I waved to her and went back to my shot. When I looked up again she was gone." Oswin said his eyes wandering over my torso.

"My chest appreciates the attention but my face is up here."

"What? Oh yes of course," he said with no noticeable change of head position.

"Did you hear anything? Anything at all?"

"Well now that you mention it. I did hear a squeal but I just thought she was enthralled by my putting ability. I have a very rare talent you know," he said.

"Yes very rare," I said.

"What did you say?" he asked as he looked towards the far corner where the Major and Felicity were entwined in what can only be described as a get a room pose. If older people want to have a love life then good for them live and let live is my motto, but did they have to do it in public. I coughed very loudly and Felicity came up for air.

"Is there anything else you need from me?" Oswin said getting closer still.

I took a deliberate side step and just managed to avoid his hand being planted on my bottom. "Not for the moment Mr Smarmer," I said, "thanks for all your help. I always say the older generation are so kind." I left him spluttering into his whiskey and returned to the office to write up the latest developments. There was a nagging feeling at the back of my brain that I had forgotten something but it wouldn't come. What wouldn't leave my head was the sight of Felicity and the Major, her claws clenched in what was left of his hair. Yuck!

The article was my best yet but it still involved someone falling asleep with our paper in the vicinity and as such would not be met with enthusiasm.

Mr De'Ath didn't carry out his promise to fire me but I was feeling at an all-time low when I went home that evening. The television couldn't distract me. Nothing on my music playlist inspired me. I couldn't settle to reading.

Exercise is not really my thing but I felt the need for something and my brain indicated that I hadn't tried a run yet. How hard could it be? After two hundred yards my body was telling me that I was an idiot. By five hundred I had stopped trying to move and was struggling to breath. I walked the rest of the block and collapsed into bed at eight; something I hadn't done since was a kid. I slept right through and woke to a breakfast of cornflakes and a cup of tea.

I went upstairs to get dressed and the next thing I knew I was sitting at my desk still in my pyjamas with a copy

of the Dibbington News made into a pirate hat perched on top
of my head.

TEN

I looked into the chocolate brown eyes of Reece Scott and I had never been so embarrassed in my life. I mean they weren't even my best pyjamas.

"Hey Care, welcome to the waking world," Reece said.

I tried to get up but my legs wouldn't support me. Reece caught me. I felt too weak to even appreciate it.

"Just sit still for a minute Care. I'd place a bet that you've been drugged," he said lowering me back into my chair.

"Can you take a blood sample maybe find out what it is?" I said.

"You sure?"

"Yes I want to find out who this psycho. It's personal now."

"That's my girl," Reece said, smiling that lazy smile again.

"I'm not your girl," I said.

"No you're not," he said. He muttered something under his breath which I didn't catch and then waved to someone outside the office.

A medical looking person came in and took out a small bag. I don't have a problem with needles as long as they stay away from my arm but I was really angry with the jerk who put me in the chair in my office in my pyjamas with a stupid hat on, and, this is the worst bit, in front of Reece Scott so I clenched my teeth and made myself watch as a sample of my blood was extracted. Once that was over I asked,

"I don't suppose anyone has any spare clothes I could borrow?"

"I have," said Mavis, our receptionist.

"We're roughly the same size but I'm afraid I was going out clubbing later. They're a bit glam for work."

"Anything has to be better than pyjamas Mavis. Thanks," I said.

I took the proffered bag to the ladies and changed into the little black dress and heels that Mavis had thought appropriate night time wear. The last time I had worn anything this feminine – well actually I can't remember ever wearing anything this feminine. I felt like that FBI agent who went in for Miss United States you know the film.

As I re-entered the office Reece had a similar expression on his face to the bloke in the movie.

"Did you just whistle?" I asked him brusquely. He shook his head and closed his mouth.

"Don't anyone say a word. I'm driving home to get some decent clothes, no offence Mavis. I'll be back soon so we can get to work on what the heck is going on here," I said, trying to maintain my dignity in three inch heels.

"Um, Care?" Reece said.

"Yes," I snapped.

"At the risk of getting my head bitten off. You can't drive anywhere until we know what that stuff in you is. I'll get someone to drive you," he looked me up and down, "better yet I'll drive you myself."

I'd thought my day couldn't possibly get worse until I tried to get out of Reece Scott's car in a skin tight short dress in those shoes. How did celebrities manage to get in and out of cars without showing their knickers? Perhaps they teach you it in stage school? Getting in was okay but the exit was a jumble of arms, legs and in betweens. I was beginning to think the pyjamas would have been a much better idea. My friendly feelings towards Mavis were rapidly disappearing.

Reece sat throughout the entire process with a look on his face that I interpreted as supressed laughter. In the end he took pity on me and held my hand as I rose from the car, balancing precariously on one leg.

"What?" I said by inelegant way of thanks.

"Nothing," Reece said.

"What? I know that look and it doesn't mean nothing."

"You scrub up well Care," he said, directing me towards the front door.

"Oh." I was nonplussed. "Er thanks."

I emerged a good ten minutes later having inexplicably taken that long to choose something to wear. I told myself it was because nothing was ironed. Lies are easier to believe if you tell them to yourself.

"Right," I said business like, "let's go catch the bad guys."

"That's my job not yours. I'm dropping you at the office," Reece said.

I sulked all the way.

ELEVEN

I'd show him. I'd solve the whole thing and be lauded by the rest of the press as a heroine. That fantasy lasted just as long as it took for me to enter the office to see several photographs of myself in pyjamas and the attractive pirate hat plastered across my door and windows. It could only be the junior reporter and janitor, who had struck up an unlikely alliance, no doubt on the basis of their intellectual equivalence. I slumped into my chair and sat to write the article of how I had been drugged and duped by the 'Snewster' as he'd been labelled by our rival paper. They would really go to town on this one.

I decided the best policy was to take the mickey out of myself before they got the chance. The trouble was, having been a victim, I was suddenly unable to see the funny side. Some person was administering a level of poison to people, and then kidnapping them, and placing them in positions of embarrassment if not danger, and then photographing them, it suddenly seemed immensely cruel and perverted. My phone rang.

"Care? It's me," a voice said.

"Oh yes and who would me be?" Well I had to pretend that my heart didn't beat a little faster at his voice, you know, play it cool.

"Don't try and be funny Care, it's Reece. I need to take your statement at the station later. It would help if you had already written down everything you can remember. I know your recall is excellent, sometimes for the most inconsequential details. I'm relying on you to be my star witness. Say two o'clock?"

He put the phone down before I could object that I had anything better to do. I mean he might arrest me for obstructing enquiries. I figured that my Mum was going to be embarrassed enough by the inevitable picture in The Times of me in my pyjamas without adding arrested to the litany of incompetence. I began writing and it flowed from me in a way that it sometimes does, particularly when the event is fresh in my mind. When I had finished and re-read it I took it to Sir for approval.

"Come in!" he yelled from somewhere underneath his desk.

"Mr De'Ath are you okay?" I peered over the top at him.

"Ow!" he said as he tried unsuccessfully to get up. He crawled a good distance from the back of the desk before he tried again.

"Just lost my pen. Gift from Mrs De'Ath. Mustn't lose," he said a little confused. Had he knocked his head harder than it had seemed?

"I brought in the article you wanted me to write. I hope it sets the right tone. Thought I'd get me before they could," I said.

"They. Right. They." He said, sitting down sharply in his chair.

"Mr De'Ath I think perhaps you'd better go home. You don't seem at all yourself."

"Myself, yes that's right, not myself."

I opened the office door.

"Mavis, could you come in for a moment?" I said. "There seems to be something wrong with Mr De'Ath. Could you phone his wife and see if she could perhaps come and get him?"

"He does look a bit of a funny colour doesn't he?" Mavis said. He had turned an unbecoming shade of grey and his head slumped onto his desk.

"Scrap the wife, phone an ambulance," I said as I tried to move him to feel for a pulse.

The pulse was there but it was fluttering, I hoped the ambulance would be quick. He might get on my nerves most of the time but I was fond of the old guy. The ambulance arrived remarkably quickly and Mavis went with him. I said I'd follow on - I wasn't sure if this had anything to do with the Snewster but I wasn't taking a chance.

"Reece it's me," I said into my phone.

"Who's me?" Reece said.

"Knock it off Scott this is serious. I think someone may have got to Mr De'Ath now as well. They've taken him to the Royal. I'll meet you there."

"I've got something to do for the next half hour but I'll be there as soon as I can. You okay Care?" Reece said.

"I'm fine but hurry," I said.

TWELVE

It turned out Mr De'Ath had a dodgy heart and that, other than the recent stress it had been put through because of the Snewster, there was nothing more sinister involved.

I attended the police station that afternoon at two, as arranged, leaving Mr De'Ath in the capable hands of his wife who terrifies me and, if the look on the consultants face was anything to go by, she felt the same way too.

Reece was polite but professional and by the time he had finished with me I felt that I never again wanted to be on the wrong side of his interrogation table. However several facts had been established which indicated further lines of enquiry to me and no doubt to him too, although you couldn't tell from his face.

Perhaps he doesn't like you after all, said a small voice in the back of my head, the one that I mostly try to ignore but who today was having her say and quite loudly too.

"Are you okay Care? I know you put out this tough image but this morning is enough to have shaken anyone," Reece said as he showed me to the door.

"I'm more angry than upset now. There are worse things than being seen in your pyjamas by your colleagues," I said. "But it's taking its toll on Mr De'Ath and it's not fair on all these poor people to have someone laughing at them."

"I always knew you were one of those principled reporters Care. Keep it up!" Reece said running his fingers through his hair and sighing before re-entering the world of police-dom.

I decided to have another word with Donna. I tracked her down at home. Her house was painted a pale pink which I found vaguely disturbing. The inside was, if anything, more disturbing. A cerise sofa with fluffy cushions and a small yappy dog on a leopard print cushion. Donna answered the door and then returned to her spot on the sofa eating chocolates and watching a chat show. I sat on the only empty chair and tried to avoid looking at the dog which was giving me the evil eye.

"Miss Smart. Can you tell me whether you remember anyone else being at the golf club for breakfast?" I said.

"Only Oswin and the waiter who served us. Then Oswin left and I was on my own."

"How long for?"

"About fifteen minutes," Donna said, still staring at the giant screen.

"Did you leave the room at all during that time?"

"No," she said, then swung round and was finally looking at me. "Actually, yes. I went to the ladies. Do you think that that's when someone drugged my food?"

"It's very possible. Have you told the police this yet?"

"No do you think I should?" She was trying to frown but the Botox wouldn't let her.

"How about you call them in the morning," I said. "I mean there's not much they can do tonight is there?"

"No you're right I'll call that lovely Detective Scott first thing," Donna said.

"You know he's married don't you," I said before my brain was properly engaged.

"Really. How interesting!" she said.

"Actually no, it's not interesting. It's the opposite of interesting. It's boring. He's boring. You should just stay away from him okay," I finished lamely.

"I see," she said. "Well, shut the door on your way out won't you."

What was that all about? Now I really would be in trouble.

Yes but you'll get an exclusive story won't you?

That'll shut Mr D. up for a bit. Oh I forgot he's in hospital.

I wonder who they've sent to replace him. I got back to the office to find the replacement clearing Mr De'Ath's desk as though he was never coming back. The man in question was the former Deputy Editor of The Dibbington Times, Reg Twine.

Life just couldn't get any more unpleasant if it tried.

THIRTEEN

Why did I have to say that?

He's assigned me to the astrology and obituary page. On the strength of my recent capture in pyjamas and unfortunate photograph in The Times. He thought that I wouldn't be up to hard reporting and I've been demoted and generally humiliated. To make it worse Donna Smartypants had a change of heart and phoned Reece Scott the second I left not only to tell him what she had told me but also that I'd told her not to tell him. Now he's not talking to me. I was at a seriously low point in my personal life and career.

Undeterred I rush through the obits and went to see if I could talk the barman into telling me the identity of the waiter who was on duty the morning Donna was Snewstered.

"I don't remember. I don't come in that early. Perhaps Duane'll know. Oy Duane?" he shouted in the direction of the veranda. A young lad who seemed to be about twelve but who held a broom like he knew what he was doing entered the bar and stood said broom against my stool.

"This lady wants to know who the waiter was on Tuesday morning. You were on weren't you?" he said.

"Yeah that's right. I don't think I'd seen him before. I told that copper who came in. I think he was from an agency. Oswin'll know which agency. You might just catch him," he said pointing out of the window to the green where I could see D. I. 'dishy' Scott talking to our resident golf pro animatedly.

Best tackle two birds with one stone was my somewhat sketchy theory as I approached Smarmer and Scott.

"Hi boys," I sounded like a bad underwear advert. Start again. "Hi men." Worse definitely worse. "Can you spare me a minute?"

"I'm off," said Reece with barely a glance in my direction, "don't forget what I said," he said to Oswin.

He walked off towards the car park and I wanted to run after him and beg his forgiveness but I would not allow myself to be humiliated in front of the Smarmer. "I suppose he's told you not to talk to me," I said.

"Yep," Oswin said.

"So you won't answer my questions."

"I didn't say that. I promised not to say anything. You can talk as much as you like," he said, "as long as I get something out of it that is."

"Like what?" I said warily.

"Like I haven't got a date to the golf club dinner on Saturday night. I hear you scrub up well."

"No way am I going with you to that."

"Okay no information for you then," he said and began to walk away.

"How about if you give me information that turns out to be useful then I'll think about it?" I said.

"No deal you'll just say it's not useful and then I'll have no date."

I was thinking hard. I really didn't want to be writing obituaries and stars for the rest of my life and I also didn't want anyone else to have to fall victim to the Snewster. On the other hand I really didn't want to go on a date with Oswin Smarmer. Perhaps I could go for a while and then leave. I mean he only said he wanted a date to go with, right, nothing about staying.

"Okay. I agree to go as your date to the golf club dinner. Now give me the information I need about the waiter which I'm sure you just gave to the police."

"Who said anything about the waiter? He was asking about Donna and whether I saw her in the breakfast room before I left."

"So who was the waiter that was on that morning? Do you know?" I asked.

"Never seen him before now but he had a birth mark on his upper left arm shaped like Australia, I saw it when his sleeve rode up as he scratched his arm," Oswin said.

"And D. I. Scott didn't ask you about this at all?"

"No. Now what time shall I pick you up Saturday?"

"What time's the dance?"

"Eight," Oswin said.

"Pick me up at seven forty five and don't be late," I said.

FOURTEEN

Although I'd agreed to go to the dance with Oswin I didn't want him getting the wrong idea so I dressed classy but definitely downbeat. Black trousers, black top not too tight and diamonds (well cubic zirconia but who can tell anyway). I wore my high heels as I wanted to feel as powerful as possible and I suspected I might meet Oswin's height with them on. I was not a little surprised when Oswin arrived at seven forty five precisely. Bonus point to the Smarmer. Oswin was in an extremely expensively cut suit and, alright, even I had to admit he looked very handsome in it.

"Good evening Ms Care. You look very lovely if a little conservative."

"Thank you. You too."

"Do I detect a softening in your attitude to me?" he said, raising his eyebrows.

"Perhaps, perhaps a little."

"A little will do for now," he said opening the car door.

I may be an independent female but I'm still a sucker for nice manners and I gratefully lowered myself into the front seat of his car and, as he closed the door, inhaled the scent of the leather interior.

The party was quiet when we arrived. The golf club had seldom looked better. The interior swathed in rich silks and velvets in deepest reds and maroons. There were fairy lights everywhere and waiters circulating with copious amounts of champagne and canapés.

Security was more obvious than usual. An extra CCTV camera had been fitted to the wall opposite the ladies and gents toilets and several looked across the veranda to the golf course beyond. The greens nearest the club house were well lit but the remainder of the course was in complete darkness.

"Drink Ms Care?" Oswin said.

"Thank you. I'll have a small glass of champagne," I said looking around to see who was already here. The Major waved from the far corner and he and Felicity made their way over to me.

"Evening. So they got you too?" the Major said.

"Yes," I said.

"I'm sorry," Felicity said with what sounded like genuine sympathy, "it's horrid really to think that they could have done anything to you while you were out of it. You know?"

The thought had occurred to me too but it didn't appear that anything had happened. The person seemed to just want to humiliate their victims as much as possible without causing them any lasting harm. That was also the police theory but I knew what Felicity meant it was the fact that anything could have happened in that time and how would any of us know.

"At least it's not just you ladies eh?" said the Major, "I mean that Brian fellow was found in the most embarrassing position wasn't he?"

I nodded half- heartedly and turned in time to see Reece Scott enter the room and on his arm the most exquisite petite blonde. By the time the Major and Felicity turned back I had gone, headed to the ladies. I couldn't let him see me like this. I mean the outfit was meant to deter Oswin Smarmer not to be out done by an ice nymphet. (Well okay she wasn't really icy-looking, that's a bit of a cliché, but I'm struggling to explain my emotions to myself let alone you!)

I dived into a cubicle. What was I going to do now? I opened my handbag searching for some kind of inspiration and noticed that I still had Mavis's dress in there. It was screwed up but was so skin tight that I figured it wouldn't make any difference once it was on. I wriggled into it, spruced up my makeup in the inadequately lit mirrors and exited the toilets looking a completely different person.

Re-entering the party it was clear that Oswin had been looking for me. He turned and promptly dropped his drink including the ice cubes down the back of some poor woman who yelped and whose companion did his best to mop her up.

Right reaction; wrong man.

FIFTEEN

Reece had noticed.

I spotted him standing in the corner with a very smug grin on his face looking in my direction and completely ignoring the blonde who was talking nineteen to the dozen and appeared not to notice his inattention. She noticed when he handed her his drink and began making his way in my direction though. If looks could kill.

"Care didn't expect you to be here. At least not in a social capacity. Who'd you come with?" Reece said casually leaning against the bar.

"That would be me," Smarmer said and placed his arm around my shoulder.

I clocked Reece's eyes narrowing at this familiarity and didn't throw the arm off as I would normally have done.

"So Smarmer how did you get Care to come to the ball with you? Blackmail?" Reece said.

I had just taken a mouthful of my drink and nearly choked on it. Oswin took this opportunity for further bodily contact and tried to administer the Heimlich manoeuvre. At which point my instincts took over and I threw him over my shoulder hard onto the floor. Reece hooted with laughter.

Oswin looked winded and then mad but rallied when Donna rushed to his side in a dress that made mine look nun like. She helped him up, shot me a look and they walked entwined to the opposite side of the room. I wasn't sure whose eyes were watering most mine or Reece's after my spluttering also turned to laughter.

"Why did you choke?" Reece finally managed.

"No reason," I said.

"Care?" he said moving closer to me.

"That trick won't work on me this time," I said.

"What trick? It's noisy in here I couldn't hear you," he said moving closer still.

"Stop it!" I said.

"Stop what. I'm not doing anything," he said. He took a lock of my hair and began winding it round and round his finger. I tried desperately not to find it seductive but was weakening and he knew it. "Care don't resist. You know you like it."

"I don't at all," I said, "I've only just washed it," I added weakly.

He grinned wolfishly and leaned in. His lips were just millimetres from mine when his whole body slammed sideways into the bar as the icy blonde landed on top of him. I tried not to laugh, really I did, but he did look so comical. My six foot police officer lying on the floor being hand-bagged by a four feet ten blonde in four inch heels.

"Get off you mad woman," he shouted trying to grab her arm as the bag came down again. It didn't work. If anything the use of the term mad made it worse.

"Did you call me mad?" she screamed, "How dare you! I'm not mad. That's what my husband used to call me. I wouldn't have answered your advert if I'd known you'd go off with the first bimbo you saw."

"Who're you calling a bimbo?" I said launching into her. Reece forgotten, we wrestled on the floor until we realised that everyone in the whole party was watching us. That brought me to a halt anyway and as I looked around she took advantage, I felt pain and everything went dark.

SIXTEEN

"Care wake up. You okay?" said a voice from far away.

Someone groaned.

"Oh good you're coming round. I was beginning to think I'd have to arrest my date on murder charges. Here let me help you sit up," the voice continued.

Where was I? The room seemed a lot smaller than I remembered it.

"You're behind the bar. It was the safest place," Reece said as he held me and pulled me to a sitting position.

"Safest? Why safest?" I said as I regained focus and saw a myriad of shelved miniature bottles.

"When you're able to stand I'll show you," Reece said holding both of my hands and smiling encouragingly.

"Ready?" he said. I nodded and launched myself ceiling-ward. I landed in his arms and stepped backwards sharply in embarrassment. He frowned but propped my elbows until I could stand on my own. The scene around me was one of minor devastation. Swathes of fabric lay, trampled and twisted. The fairy lights remained but cast a spooky glow over the mangled mess that was upturned trays of canapés and drinks. Broken glasses shattered where they fell and a hat stand poked out of the front of the trophy cabinet.

"I really don't remember making this much mess," I said.

"You didn't. Sophie did," Reece said.

"The blonde?" I said.

He nodded.

"Where'd you get her from?" I said.

"I thought I'd kill two birds with one stone. I've been investigating a blackmailer who's been advertising in the personals. I answered an ad and invited her here. I thought I could take another look at the scene of at least two of the Snewster's crimes and find out if she was the blackmailer at the same time."

"And is she?" I said.

"No idea!" he said. We both grinned.

"Where is she now?"

"Warming one of our cells. She may or may not be a blackmailer but she assaulted at least three people including you and trashed the place; as you can see."

"Well at least you upped your arrests this month."

"There is that I suppose. We're looking at her house now. If she is the blackmailer it may almost have been worth it."

"My head doesn't agree," I said placing my hand gingerly to my temple.

"You ought to get checked over by the paramedic. They're in the hallway with the Major, he got caught in the crossfire when Felicity waded in on Sophie after she'd whacked you. It was quite a scene."

"Shame I missed it," I said, "where's Oswin?"

"Left before the fight, with Donna; hasn't been seen since," Reece said, "I'll drop by on them both tomorrow morning. For the moment, Care, let's get you home shall we?"

I didn't have the strength to argue. The paramedic gave me the once over and in the absence of any dizziness or blurred vision said I could go as long as there would be someone with me all night. Reece assured him that this wouldn't be a problem and squeezed my upper arm so tightly when I started to object that I yelped.

When we got outside I began, "You are not staying the night at my house."

"Oh yes I am. Doctors' orders," Reece said opening the passenger door.

"What if I say no," I folded my arms across my chest.

"I will simply restrain you and take you to A&E, for your own good."

"Humph!"

"What was that Care? Were you perchance agreeing wholeheartedly with my excellent suggestion?" I didn't answer but sat down in the passenger seat and allowed him to close the car door behind me.

I know what you're thinking but nothing happened, I slept in my bed, he on the sofa.

SEVENTEEN

I woke up the next morning much earlier than usual.

There was a noise coming from downstairs and the unmistakable smell of toast. My stomach gave a loud growl and I rolled out of bed and into a pair of jeans and T- shirt which were on the floor but looked vaguely crease free.

"Morning, Care," Reece said as I poked my head round the kitchen door.

I couldn't help thinking that no one had the right to look so groomed and wrinkle-less after spending the night on the couch. "Morning. That smells delicious," I said, "I'm fairly certain that I didn't have any bread in the house though."

"Just popped down the shops. You now have bread, butter, Marmite and milk. Are you a Marmite person?" Reece said as he put two more slices of bread in the toaster and then slathered butter on two further bits. If this is his idea of breakfast then I think I might be in love, said one half of my brain before I could gain control over it. The other half was firmly fixed on the toast and butter and my stomach again emitted a Vesuvian eruption.

"I'll take that as a yes. Here, get that down you Care. I want you fit and well today. You're going to have to give me another statement and then I'm keeping you with me for the rest of the day in case anything else happens to you. You can write an article on a day with a policeman. It'll be fun," Reece said. I was too besotted to object. Whether with Reece or the toast was a close call; a man who feeds you is just so attractive.

First stop was the police station where I gave an official statement. The only tricky moment was when the constable with Reece asked why they had me on CCTV, going into the ladies in one outfit and exiting in another. Reece turned and gave me his full interrogative stare which I returned, but it was my gaze that lowered first. I still hadn't told Reece about the man with the birth mark and was beginning to feel guilty about it. Besides, the way things were with the temporary editor I would never get the chance to do another exclusive.

Next up Oswin and Donna. We tried first one then the other of their houses and when that failed we went back to the golf club. The barman said they were on the course, Donna was now officially taking lessons and they had left about an hour ago. Reece commandeered a buggy and we set off in search.

"So Care why exactly did you get changed?" Reece said.

I squirmed but said nothing.

"That was about the time that Sophie and I arrived wasn't it?" he said.

"Look isn't that them over there?" I said spotting the plunging red crossover top and skin tight Capri pants of Donna Smart.

"Yes that's them. I bet you could see that top from Mars," Reece said.

"It's a very similar colour I believe" I said.

Reece laughed then muttered under his breath. "Don't think a change of subject will help. I'm determined to get to the bottom of the costume change you know. Donna, Oswin, glad I've caught you. Can we have a quick chat about last night?"

EIGHTEEN

"Well they didn't give much away did they?" Reece said half an hour later, "but unless they are in cahoots it lets them both off the hook."

"Wish they hadn't gone into quite so much detail though," he said, steering the golf cart back to the club house. As we arrived I spotted Felicity and the Major at the bar and went over to thank Felicity for her help last evening and to see how the Major was.

"Oh it was nothing," Felicity said fanning herself with a magazine, "I mean she was so trashy. What was your dishy Sergeant doing with her anyway?"

"He's not my sergeant," I said. "I think it might have been to do with work."

"Ooh! Is she a criminal? How exciting? I've never met a real one before," Felicity said, "well except the one that did that thing to me."

"I know I keep forgetting too. It's horrible isn't it?"

"Yes my dear it is and it simply must stop. It looks so comical from the outside but it doesn't feel like that on the inside does it?"

I bade the pair farewell and decided that now was the time to come clean about the birth marked man. It would get me and Oswin into trouble but I was feeling the full weight of the omission. Reece was sitting in the bar talking to one of his constables who was overseeing the final clear up from the night before.

"What's up Care? You decided to come clean about the costume change?" Reece said. I must have looked as worried as I felt because he said, "It's alright Care. I'm only teasing. I know why and I'm flattered, honestly. I'm really flattered," he said placing his hand gently on my shoulder.

Ten minutes later- "I'll drop you off at home," Reece said.

"But….." I said.

"No buts. You've put yourself and other people in danger Care. Next time tell me everything," Reece said as he drove off and I entered my house dejected. Reece was angry with me but after a sleep and with the darkness came a steely clarity. This was not my fault. It was the Snewsters and I was going to nail him if it was the last thing I did. I would do it not just for me but for Felicity, Donna and Brian and for Reece. I would show him that I was the sort of person he thought I was. I would start first thing in the morning.

But I couldn't sleep. The moon was shining through the gap in my curtains. It sounded like next door's cat was fighting with a pigeon in their back garden and the milkman was trying to be quiet and consequently making more noise.

I was wide awake.

I picked up the torch that I keep at the side of my bed. It's more for protection than light, I do have electricity. The cat decided at that moment to go in for the kill and it sounded like the pigeon pecked at the cat's eyes as it let out a mighty yowl and then silence.

I dropped the torch on the floor in fright and it rolled under my bed. I initially felt for it but it had rolled too far in so I had to crawl under the bed. This was tricky as my front half was becoming wedged the further in I went. I could see the outline of something long and round on the opposite side and just as it occurred to me that I would be better off getting out and going to the other side to access it I felt something small and round dig me in the ribs. I pocketed whatever it was and then extracted myself and reached the torch easily from the other side.

I switched on the bedroom light and pulled the mystery object from my pocket.

It was nail varnish. Passionate Peony.

NINETEEN

The remembrance of waking at the office in my pyjamas overtook me. I became scared and then very angry. Brian Weatherall had had this exact shade of nail varnish in his bedroom. The only other items of significance had been a couple of receipts from a local café. My plan of action now had a starting place.

Stone's café was a greasy spoon. Not where I would have expected to find Brian Weatherall. He had struck me as a man who took care to be seen in all the best places. This was not of the best. I pushed open the front door and a bell announced my presence to the proprietor.

"Yeah," said a voice from somewhere behind a ribbon curtain.

"Excuse me, I'm looking for the owner," I said flashing my card at an emaciated elderly man with a huge nose and perfectly balanced glasses. He looked at me over their rim suspiciously.

"What d'you want?"

"I wanted to know if you had seen this man in here recently," I said proffering a photograph of Brian that I'd asked our photographer to take to accompany our first article about the Snewster.

"What if I have?" he said.

I passed a twenty pound note over the counter and ordered a pie.

"Well now, he comes in quite regular, or at least he did until about three weeks ago."

"Was he on his own?"

"No used to come in with some common looking woman," he said.

"What did she look like exactly?"

"You know common looking. Bleached blonde hair, perma-tan, skirts up to her backside and bright red talons," he said.

"Did he mention her name?" I said hopefully.

"Nah. I wasn't listening. I thought it a bit odd that he was in here. He looked out of place if you know what I mean."

"And you haven't seen either of them for about three weeks?"

"I said I hadn't seen him. She comes in every Thursday regular as clockwork. Orders a cheese and onion pasty and coleslaw, always the same."

"Well thanks for your help. If you think of anything else would you give me a call? Or if she happens to come in early," I said slipping him another twenty with my card.

"I'll be sure to give you a call," he said and disappeared through the doorway once more.

Gulping in the smell of fresh air outside, I binned the remainder of the pie and made my way to the tennis club. Brian was holding court amongst his usual harem of late middle agers. I approached. They ignored me. I coughed and their cackles rose in volume. Brian, a naturally polite person, eventually managed to extricate himself from their attentions.

"So sorry Miss Care. I'm rather embarrassed but they won't leave me alone," he said.

"I understand," I said, (although really, I didn't).

"How can I help?" he said.

"I've just been to Stone's café."

"Oh yes?" There was no change to his expression so I ploughed on.

"It's just that I found a pot of nail varnish at my house after I was taken," I held up my bitten nails, "I don't wear any."

"So I see," he said, "what's that got to do with me?"

"The lady you were with at the café had crimson talons."

"I expect half of the ladies over there have too," he said.

"Well actually they mostly have pale pink or French. I looked."

"Okay so she has red finger nails. I ask again what has that to do with me?"

I couldn't admit that I'd found the same bottle at his place because I wasn't supposed to have been there but I didn't think I'd need to. I could see the cogs whirring in his brain. He knew exactly why I was asking these questions and when he went to meet her I would follow.

TWENTY

He took his time. I watched several tennis matches, looked up my horoscope on my phone and called my best friend for a chat.

Two hours later he emerged from the main entrance, climbed into his convertible and drove in the direction of the café. I was expecting him to park outside it but he went past and turned right into a road of terraced houses. He pulled onto a driveway about halfway down on the left and I pulled into a parking space about fifty metres further on the right. By the time I'd made my way back to the house he'd disappeared.

I don't like loitering outside houses. Generally there is some nosey parker who'll call the police, so I've learned to enter the surroundings of the property and find my own hiding place inside.

The opportunity for discovery here was huge. It was a tiny front garden with no shrubbery or trees. I wandered along the road to the end of the block which thankfully did not run the entire length of the street. There was a gateway which on inspection led to an alleyway which ran the entire length of the block. A line of bins gave me the location of the house and I stopped outside number sixteen which had been neatly stencilled on the top of said bin.

I listened carefully and could hear voices coming from the house. The kitchen window was open and I could hear Brian's voice clearly.

"What's going on Audrey?" he said.

"I don't know what you mean Brian. I ain't been nowhere near no nosey reporter's house," Audrey said.

"I didn't tell you she was a reporter," Brian said.

"Now there's no need for that Brian." Audrey's voice raised a tone or two, "I ain't been near her I swear."

"You better be telling the truth Audrey. We've been through this before. You can't keep spooking my girlfriends it's not on."

Girlfriends! What was he on about? The very idea made me slightly nauseous. I think I might be coming down with something. Nearly missed what he said next.

"Don't make me go to the police Audrey."

"Please don't for Ian's sake."

"You can't keep playing that card Audrey. It won't work for ever," Brian's voice sounded tired.

"He's still your son i'n't he?"

"Yes of course he is and I support him, but you've got to get it through your head we're not a couple any more. We haven't been for years," Brian said.

"Oh now you don't mean that Brian. How about a cuppa?"

"No I'm going. Please, please let me be Audrey."

I stayed very still until I heard him leave. I never thought in a million years that I'd feel sorry for Brian especially after the girlfriend comment but Audrey was clearly nuts. I had to get in the house. Audrey had talons of the sharp and red nature but I'm not an expert on nail varnish shades.

It was the sort of neighbourhood where everyone knew everyone. Five minutes later I had a stroke of luck. Audrey went out into the front garden and started talking to the lady next door. Their conversation settled into what could only be described as a good gossip

I took my chance and nipped in the open back door. The bathroom seemed the obvious place to start. I was just headed for the stairs when I noticed that this was the older type of house where the bathroom was on the ground floor. A quick glance round showed me a medicine cabinet and two dusty looking shelves.

Nothing on the shelves. I could hear Audrey still talking.

Medicine cabinet. Bingo! Passionate peony. Deposited in pocket. Dash for the back door. Too late.

"Who are you and what are you doing in my kitchen?"

TWENTY-ONE

Not Audrey.

A fifteen year old boy, large for his age, at a guess Ian?

"Ah Ian good to meet you I was just visiting on the off chance of catching your mother. I've just been to see your father. I hoped to clarify something he said."

"I know who you are. You're a hit on the internet. There's a photo of you in your pyjamas," he said, suddenly very much resembling his father.

"Yes funny that," I said looking round for a way out before Audrey came back, "anyway got to go."

"I thought you said you wanted to speak with my Mum."

"Yeah well I can see she's busy. I'll come back later," I said and fairly ran out of the door and vaulted across the back wall. I hadn't gone very far when the sirens sounded behind me and a car pulled up.

"Care, what are you doing here?" said a familiar voice.

"Me, oh just a coincidence. You know," I said vaguely.

"I suspect I do know. There was a report of an intruder at number sixteen matching your description. Matching it exactly," Reece said.

"Really?" I said playing for time.

"Really. Down to the colour of your pyjamas on that internet picture. An explanation if you please," Reece said.

I was going to answer, him, honestly I was, but the sheer arrogance of his tone made me stop. How dare he? Who did he think he was? Ten minutes later I found out as I was handcuffed and taken to the police station for questioning.

"Reece, please, I was only going there to talk to her. I was following up the story on Brian and her name popped up," I said.

(What? I wasn't exactly lying.)

"Popped up when you questioned the man at the café?" Reece said.

How did he find out about that? "But he said he didn't know her name."

"Benefits of having a badge," Reece said, "I was on my way to the house when the call came in."

If I told him about the nail varnish he'd have to charge me with theft. But if he found it for himself. I bet she had more than one pot. I needed to tell him about the nail varnish at my house. I needed to come clean. "I didn't tell you but I found a pot of nail varnish at my house after I returned home to change," I said.

"I remember you getting changed," Reece said a smile playing at the corner of his mouth.

"Well it was there when I went up. I forgot to tell you about it," I said.

"It's not yours then."

"Not mine, no. Perhaps one of our other victims might have found the same thing at their house?" I said.

"Interpretation – you know that they did," Reece said.

"Did you find any anywhere else?" he said.

"I found some in my pocket," I said.

"Before or after you dropped in on Audrey and her son?" Reece said.

"Might have been after I suppose. I'm struggling to remember. You know I think the drugging the other day might have had some side effects. Perhaps I need to go home and have a lie down."

"Nice try Care. You're coming with me to each of the victims' houses. I will not be letting you out of my sight," Reece said.

What was a girl reporter to do? I followed and tried to look like I didn't like it.

TWENTY-TWO

Donna was obviously pleased to see Reece but her expression changed when she saw me behind him. I didn't take it personally Donna was the sort who saw every man as a challenge and every woman as a rival.

"You want to see my nail varnish collection?" Donna repeated.

"Yes," said Reece, "please."

"Okay. Follow me," she said and led us into a bedroom even fluffier and pinker than the downstairs would have led me to believe. If I had a cerise cushion covered in feathers I would have bits of feather all over my clothing. How did Donna manage to wear white trousers and not get a single strand on her?

"I'd be grateful if you could wait outside," Reece said already ushering her to the door. As he closed it he indicated that I should begin searching her dressing table while he looked about on the floor, under the bed and in the bedside cabinets.

"Nothing on the floor that I can see," he said, "it's remarkably neat and tidy given the excess of femininity."

"This kind of femininity doesn't preclude tidiness just taste," I said.

"You really should learn to temper that tongue of yours, Care. It'll get you into trouble one day."

"Not today," I said waving a small crimson bottle in his direction.

"Are we sure it's not hers?" he asked.

"If it is, it's the only bottle in her collection that isn't some shade of pale pink."

"Let's go and ask her shall we," Reece said, "after you."

"It isn't mine!" Donna said.

"Have you seen it before?" Reece said.

"Now that you mention it, yes. I noticed it yesterday but I just thought maybe Oswin brought it over to mark his golf balls or something," she grinned smugly in my direction.

Dear Lord, she actually thought that I was jealous of her and Smarmer. I returned the smile also a little smugly.

"We'll ask him," Reece said, "and we'll be taking this with us. Thank you for your time."

"My pleasure," Donna said and leaned over to kiss him on the cheek. Reece accepted the kiss without comment and left. Donna snuck a look in my direction and smiled sweetly. Okay, this time she got me. I would be very surprised if I hadn't turned green.

"Where next?" I said.

"Felicity's," Reece said.

"Oh great, more Bertie Wertie," but then I remembered the way Felicity had jumped on Sophie at the golf club dance.

"Be nice," Reece said.

"I'm always nice." We drove in silence to Felicity's house. She wasn't home.

"Golf club," we said together.

Felicity and the Major were ensconced at their usual table and it looked as if they may have had a few alcoholic beverages inside them. Otherwise there was no possible excuse for their pawing each other in such a manner.

Be nice Care!

Reece coughed discreetly.

"Ah Scott. Wondered when you'd be getting back to us. Any progress on catching this scoundrel?" said the Major.

"Some yes," Reece said taking a seat across from them; I joined him.

"Good, good, that's the fellow," the Major said placing a heavy hand on Felicity's knee. She didn't as much as flinch. Maybe she loved the old bloke after all.

Reece turned to Felicity and said "I need to ask Mrs Thorp whether she has gained any new nail varnishes in the past few days."

"Nail varnish!" said the Major, "what's that got to do with anything?"

"Hush now Bertie. I'm sure Detective Inspector Scott has his reasons. Well, now you mention it, yes I found a bottle of some disgusting colour, putrid poppy was it? On my dressing table."

"Did you happen to keep it?" Reece said.

"Actually I was intending to throw it away but then Bertie turned up and I popped it inside my handbag. Here let me have a look," she said rummaging through her capacious Tote bag. "Yes here it is. Passionate peony, not putrid poppy." She handed the bottle to Reece who took it from her with gloved hands and into an evidence bag. The Major and Felicity were dying to ask what this was about but Reece's countenance stopped any enquiry.

We were just standing to leave when there was a disturbance in the corridor and Brian Weatherall burst into the room. "What the hell do you mean by harassing my son?" he said looking directly at me.

TWENTY-THREE

I'm a coward by nature and hid behind the only law enforcer in the room.

Reece stepped aside and let Brian through to me, watching carefully.

"You followed me and then spoke to my ex and my son. What have they got to do with any of this? Eh? Answer me," Brian said.

I froze. I had done all that he accused me of, what was I supposed to say? I didn't expect what I did say.

"I'm sorry," I said, "I just wanted to find out who did this to us. I didn't really think any further than that."

Brian deflated like a balloon. He sat on a stool opposite Felicity and the Major.

"Waiter!" Reece said, "Whiskey here please."

The waiter returned quickly and Reece handed him the glass.

"Sorry for that unforgiveable display," Brian said taking a sip. "I've tried so long to keep my two lives separate I just got angry."

"Why did you try and keep them separate?" asked Felicity.

"I was embarrassed ……….. of them. Now I'm embarrassed of me," Brian said.

Felicity walked over and placed her arm round his shoulders. "We've all done things we're embarrassed about. It's what we do once we realise our mistake that counts."

"Thank you but I really don't know what I can do to make up for ignoring a fifteen year old most of his life; however I felt about his mother," Brian said.

"Well you could start by going over and seeing them and reassuring them about the lady who came to visit them and her motives," Reece said.

"Yes. I understand that, at least. I hope you catch them soon," Brian downed his whisky and started to get up.

"Before you go Brian did you find any nail varnish in your home after the incident at the golf club?" Reece said.

"Not that I remember. I hate the stuff - Audrey used to have every colour under the sun. I threw it all out when she left."

"Never mind. Thanks and drive carefully," Reece said. To the Major and Felicity, "Well we'd better be going. Thanks for all your help."

In the car his mood changed. "I'm beginning to have an idea about these kidnappings."

"Are you?" I said. I remained completely clueless. Some investigative reporter I was. "Mr De'Ath will be very pleased to hear it."

"How is he?" Reece asked.

"On the mend. His wife spoke with Mavis yesterday. They don't know when he'll be back at work though."

"I thought you'd be pleased he was off," Reece said.

"That was pre - Reg I didn't think it could get worse than Mr D. I was wrong. So what are we doing now?" The car swung round into my road. I hadn't noticed.

"We, are doing nothing. I, am going to see a man about a dog."

"Is that a euphemism?"

"Take it as you will," he said and drove off at a lick.

I trudged up to my front door shoulders somewhere around my waist. I was enjoying my moment of detecting and particularly the detective. I put the key in the lock, felt a cloth over my mouth and the world became fuzzy, then dark.

TWENTY-FOUR

I could smell lavender and diesel. Not an unpleasant combination in itself but confusing to a bruised brain. My next thought was why me? No one else had been taken twice. But this felt different.

I opened my eyes slowly and they might as well have remained shut for all the difference it made. I hadn't been scared the last time. I was terrified now.

I was afraid to reach out my hands as I had no idea what I might encounter, but gradually the fear of not moving and never getting out of wherever I was overcame me. To the left was something soft, velvety which went upwards – a curtain. To the right - nothing. I tried to shuffle along on my bottom but immediately realised that my belt had been looped round something heavy, a chair? A table? Not the sort that could be easily moved. In fact it appeared to be bolted to the floor.

The café.

Hadn't seen that one coming. I couldn't make out whether it was dark because it was night time or dark because the shutters were down. Whatever it was I was alone. I could always tell when I was alone it was just a feeling but I was never wrong.

Except when I was wrong.

I could hear breathing. Well, actually panting to be more accurate, and it was coming from in the corner. "Hello!" I called. "Is there anybody there?"

Okay, even to myself I sounded like a cheap horror movie but give me a break; I was in the dark here. (I know, enough with the clichés.) My brain was in a clench and, speaking of clenching, the lemonade that I'd had at the golf club earlier had worked its way through my system and I desperately needed the little girls' room.

"Hello," I tried again, "I was just wondering if I could use the toilet. I don't want to make a mess on the floor and thought you could perhaps untie me just my legs so I could ….you know."

The panting stopped briefly, I heard a rattling sound and the room was flooded with sunlight. A figure with a rounded belly rushed towards me and began undoing the bindings.

"Thank God! Please", I said urgently, "where's the bathroom?"

A hand pulled me up and dragged me to the back of the store and into a room which looked like a cloakroom and I was shoved unceremoniously into the rather grubby toilet. When I plucked up the courage to unlock the bathroom door I finally saw who had rescued me and it wasn't who I'd thought. Audrey's son Ian stared back at me with his big trusting eyes.

"You okay?" he said.

"Yeah, thanks. Sorry about that," I said. "Did you see anyone else about at all?" I added walking over to the ribboned door and peering out into the café.

"Nah came in to unlock for opening and found you there. Gave me quite a fright really," Ian said looking at my wrists that were still tied up with what looked like a tent guy rope.

"I better call the police I suppose," I said non-commitally.

"Yeah," he wasn't keen either, "could we just wait maybe until the early morning rush is over that's when we have our best sales."

I sighed. I was sorely tempted to say yes but the cricket on my shoulder was fairly screaming at me 'look what happened last time you left the police out of the loop.' "Sorry Ian. I'm gonna have to call them," I said as I reached for my mobile, it wasn't there.

"Can I use the phone in the office?" I said.

"Help yourself. I've got to take the delivery in a moment. Police eat a lot don't they," his face brightened.

Perhaps on the television but this isn't a doughnut shop in New York. I made the call and to my frustration Reece wasn't in and without my mobile phone I didn't have his number. I spoke to his desk sergeant and reported the crime, they said they'd send someone along as soon as they could.

Ian was lifting in crates of food from the back door. I offered to help. Well, there are worse places to have to wait for the police than a café. When he'd finished I asked for a coffee and a tea cake and sat back to wait.

I know I've made myself sound really cool and collected but that is the joy of being a journalist; I can embellish the truth. I was, in fact absolutely freaked out by what had just happened with no idea why I had been taken, and even more puzzlingly left to be found. I managed to hold it together, just about, in front of Ian but as soon as I saw Reece's head exiting his sergeant's car outside I began shaking and I just couldn't stop.

"Miss, Miss would you like some sweet tea, I can get you some just wait until I've served Phil here and I'll be with you," Ian said from behind the counter.

Phil duly served; Ian placed the tea on the table like he was making an offering to the Gods. The doorbell rang and my policeman strode across the room. Ian genuflected and disappeared back into his enclave.

"Hey Care, I said I'd have to stick to you like glue. I should have listened to my own advice," Reece said.

"I can look after myself," I said and promptly burst into tears.

He pulled me up and into a hug.

"Tell me what happened," he said lowering me into my seat and crouching on those terribly long legs to be at my level.

"There's not much to tell really. You drove off, I turned round to unlock my front door and someone shoved a cloth over my mouth. Next thing I know I wake up here. My hands were tied with a piece of cord that looks a bit of tent rope and I've got a pounding headache. That's it."

"But why?" Reece said.

"Quite. As far as I can tell nothing else has happened to me except my phone being missing," I hesitated as a thought struck me, "has anyone checked my house?" I stood up too quickly and the blood rushed to my head. The room swam and I sat back down with a thump.

"Perhaps I should try that again, but slowly," I said.

Reece went to take my arm and my pride took over.

"I'm fine. See," I said suppressing any urge to sway.

"Fine. Right. Sergeant let's go."

As we piled into the car, I waved to Ian in thanks. He tipped two fingers in salute and went back to serving the long line of builders.

TWENTY-FIVE

It looked normal from the outside. Reece took the key from me, indicating that I should stay behind his sergeant. He pushed the door and poked his head through.

"Hallway looks clear."

With a flick of his head he told the sergeant to go into the living room while he made his way, with me following, into the kitchen. All looked calm, well normal anyway - housework not being a priority. Trying to ignore Reece's look of faint disgust at the sight of my kitchen sink I surreptitiously swept a few items into the bin.

"Don't touch Care. It's evidence. Clearly they've been in and trashed the place," Reece said his eyes going to the pile of papers in the corner by the back door.

"Yes, clearly," I agreed.

"Inspector," called the sergeant from the living room. There was something in his tone that made the hairs on the back of my neck stand to attention.

It was horrid.

Someone had placed a shop mannequin in the middle of the room, it was dressed in Mavis's black dress and it had a photograph of my face sellotaped to the head. Across the body a piece of paper was taped and, in red letters, the words 'Back off bitch'. Reece turned towards me. Perhaps he expected me to burst into tears again but this time I was furious. Someone had broken into my house, invaded my privacy and threatened me. I was beyond incensed, I was incandescent with fury.

"Care? Try and remain calm and don't touch anything," Reece said, "Sergeant seal off the room and call forensics. This looks like an amateur job, maybe they've been sloppy. Care with me."

"I'm not your oppo," I said marching towards my own car before realising that I had no keys, no money, no phone. I turned round and Reece was watching me with arms folded.

"Why d'you have to be so stubborn Care? We can work this out together. I didn't listen to my own advice once and look what happened. I'm not making the same mistake again."

I too folded my arms. " 'kay," I said sulkily.

"Right we'd better check on the others," Reece said.

" 'kay," I said again, aware that I sounded like a sulky teenager but I couldn't seem to help myself. "Brian?" I ventured.

"Donna," he said.

Donna, huh!

We sat in silence in front of Donna's house. It looked quiet as if no one was up but suddenly she came out of the front door looking agitated and began banging on her neighbours door. Reece was out of the car and across to her before I could undo my seat belt.

He spoke to her and then held her shoulders as she gestured at her front door. By the time I was out of the car Donna's neighbour was taking her in and I was left standing in the middle of the street like a dummy. Bad choice of words.

"Care stay outside. It's not something you want to see," Reece paused, "again."

"Same as mine," I deduced. He nodded and went back to the car radioing in for assistance.

"Felicity!" I said.

"I've already asked a couple of my P.C.'s to check her house. They haven't got back to me yet."

"Who the hell is doing this?" I said my anger petering out leaving me feeling deflated and tired.

"I don't know but they're beginning to get careless."

"They are?" I couldn't see it myself, they were definitely getting more deranged and I felt they were more dangerous, but careless, no.

Reece was in full work mode and I no longer existed. You would think he would be too busy to notice me slinking off but you'd be wrong. I tried but he grabbed my shoulder none too gently and indicated that I may wish to take a seat in the front of the police car; then he locked the door.

"That's police harassment! False imprisonment! You can't do this to me," I shouted.

"It's police protection," he said, "I can't do my job and worry about you at the same time."

That shut me up. I was fairly certain that there was a compliment in there somewhere. Damn him.

A disembodied voice spoke from the dashboard. "Inspector?"

I banged on the window. Reece waved his hand in dismissal.

"Inspector?" again.

I banged on the window and just kept on banging until he finally looked round and I could see his mouth form the word, "What?!" I pointed towards the dashboard. That got his attention, finally.

"What did you think I was attracting your attention for?" I yelled as he opened the door.

"With you Care I never know," Reece said before answering the voice.

I refolded my arms carefully and glared at his profile.

"It's the same at Felicity's Inspector," said the dashboard voice.

"Seal it off. As soon as the team have finished here I'll send them over. We haven't got enough people to deal with this all at once," Reece said, "stay on guard and I'll see if we can call in anyone off duty."

I looked at his face. "You're worried."

He nodded. "I thought he was getting careless and he is but he's dangerous too. Although not so much towards you it seems. Why would that be?"

I shrugged, how was I to know? My brain was still a little foggy from whatever I'd been drugged with. I couldn't think properly.

"Perhaps he has a soft spot for you? Who do we know who has a soft spot for you?" he said looking at me in a way that was far too intrusive for my liking.

"I'm drawing a blank," I said.

"Well I'm not but I can deal with him later," Reece said and turned back towards the house.

"Hey what about me?" I said to the air.

An hour later he was back and we were on our way to Felicity's. The pattern was repeated. I was locked in the car while he checked that everything that could be done was being done.

"Right, now for Smarmer," Reece said as he lowered himself back into the driver's seat.

I nearly choked on thin air. "Smarmer! Why him?"

"Because he blackmailed you for a date," Reece said taking an amber light at some speed.

"But it can't be him," I said.

"Why not?"

It was a good question and all of a sudden I wasn't so sure. He had been at the golf club for at least two of the incidents and we only had his word for the waiter with the birth mark shaped like Australia. He was strong enough and creepy enough. I wish I could remember something about who had attacked me. Could I remember anything that would help?

Reece, in the uncanny way he has, mirrored my thoughts, "Can you remember anything at all about the person who attacked you? A smell? A feel? Did you see their fingers as they put the cloth over your mouth? Did you manage to react at all? Damage him in any way?"

I was trying to remember but everything around it was a big blur.

"Run through it with me again out loud. It might help," Reece said as we pulled into the golf club car park.

"I said goodbye to you. Saw you drive off. Turned round to find my keys in my bag and someone shoved a cloth over my mouth and that's it," I said.

"Concentrate on their hands. Were they male or female? Did they smell?"

I frowned in concentration there must be something. "The smell was sweet but mixed with something else."

I had a sudden image of the hand and a flash of red.

TWENTY-SIX

"I think they had nail varnish on. It might have been fresh on, you know that astringent smell," I said.

Reece leaned back. "Not personally no but I believe it's a bit like cellulose. Damn, it's beginning to look like a woman," he said.

"Why?"

"Well nail varnish," Reece said casually looking at his own nails.

"Hey just because you don't wear it doesn't mean men don't. I never thought you were so narrow-minded," I said smiling as he squirmed in his seat.

"Okay supposing you're right. But Smarmer?!"

"Why not?"

Reece looked across at the windows of the club house and as I followed his gaze I could see Oswin chatting to yet another well-heeled lady of indeterminate age. As she turned I couldn't help from exclaiming,

"No!"

"What?" Reece said, looking at my jaw-dropped face.

"It's Mrs De'Ath," I said before he gently closed my mouth with one finger.

"Let's go and say hello then," he said and we both walked across to the clubhouse doors.

It was crowded in the reception area as a coachload of tourists had just arrived and it sounded like they were here for lessons en masse. By the time we'd fought our way through them Oswin was already by the receptionist's side, making a well- rehearsed speech about course rules and health and safety.

Reece strode towards him not to be deterred by the crowd and I took the opportunity to pin down Mrs De'Ath at the bar. Judging by the size of her gin and tonic she either had something to celebrate or drown.

"Phyllis dear whatever are you doing here?" she said giving me the double air kiss.

"Oh you know. The usual journalist stuff," I said taking the seat beside her.

"Has someone died?" she said stirring her drink vigorously.

"Died?"

"I thought you were doing obituaries now?"

"Yes, yes I am," I resisted grinding my teeth, "so how's Mr D?"

As I finished my sentence the floodgates opened and she downed the G & T in one. "He's left me."

"He's what?" I said before I could help it, then more sympathetically, "but we thought he was in hospital."

"He was but I went to see him yesterday afternoon and he'd checked out in the company of some tart."

Small bells began ringing. "Tart? What kind of tart?" I said glancing across at Reece who was still talking to Oswin.

"Brassy blonde. Big chest, low cut blouse, crimson talons."

Alarm bells.

"I mean he used to hate me painting my nails even pale colours; liked them natural. Now he leaves me for someone like that. I mean I don't know what to do. How could he?" she said shaking her glass at the barman for another.

I placed my hand on her arm. "Mrs De'Ath," I said.

"Call me June dear," she said.

"June. It may not be quite as you think. Come with me," I said and taking her hand led her out into the foyer.

Reece came over leaving Smarmer to his coach party.

"I don't think it's him," he whispered, "he's been here almost constantly today and his story can be confirmed by dozens of witnesses."

I pulled him to one side and told him what June had said,

"It sounds just like Audrey," I said, "and if it is,

Mr D. is probably in danger."

He turned.

"Mrs De'Ath, your husband, when did he leave the hospital exactly?"

"The nurse said about four."

"I'd like to speak with that nurse. Care you're with me," Reece said, "Mrs De'Ath is there anywhere you could go so that you're not alone?"

"My sister's. I'll give you the number. Call me if you find him. Then I can kill him."

Reece raised his eyebrows. She laughed nervously.

"I think you might have had too much to drink to drive. I'll get the receptionist to call you a taxi," Reece said crossing to the desk.

"We'll find him Mrs D. I promise," I said.

"Thank you Phyllis. You always were a good girl. You should take a chance with that nice young man," she said and headed back towards the bar. At my stern look she shrugged and said, "If I'm getting a taxi one more won't hurt."

Right. Wishing I could join her I trailed after Reece. When did I become a police assistant? What happened to strong independent woman? On the other hand hanging onto Reece's tails had its advantages, first on the scene, personal police protection, two brains better than one. Plus you fancy him said my traitorous inner voice.

We were in luck, the nurse was on day shifts at the moment and was back on duty. Reece and I used the lift to get to the third floor and found her behind the desk.

"That's right he checked out yesterday. Actually now you question it, it was a bit funny. He wasn't his usual self. You work for him don't you?" directed at me.

I nodded.

"You'll know what I mean then, real docile he was and her – well, having seen the missus I was surprised but sometimes men like their bits on the side to be different to their wives don't they?"

"What if we said that she may not have been his mistress? We think he might have been taken against his will," I said, earning me a pointed look from Reece. If we took the route he was taking we'd be here all day, I'd seen cop shows before.

The nurse considered this and you could see the thought settle in her brain and then enlightenment. "Well now, that would explain it," she said waving her pen around, "he kept pawing at her in a quite ungentlemanly way but I just thought he couldn't wait to get her alone, if you know what I mean. Well now they always say you shouldn't judge a book by its cover don't they?"

"Quite," Reece said, "did she by any chance say where they were going?"

"No although she said something about it being a nice day and he'd enjoy being outside."

"Thanks for your help," Reece said.

I'm competitive by nature and wanted to come up with where they might be before him so his next words took me by surprise,

"Let's get back to the station."

"But Mr De'Ath," I said, "he's in danger. She's mad, she might hurt him."

"I don't think so," Reece said.

"You better be right 'cos I'm not explaining to Mrs D. why her husband has been boiled like a bunny," I said.

"You're so dramatic Care. No wonder you write such exacting fiction."

TWENTY-SEVEN

Turned out Reece wasn't sitting back and waiting for Mr D to die. As soon as we were in the car he radioed for all local police to look out for him and gave such an accurate description of Audrey's quirks and attributes that I couldn't help thinking that he was the one who should be composing fiction for a living.

The reason for going back to the station became clear when we pulled up and I saw Brian leaning against his car smoking a cigarette. He stubbed it out when he saw us arrive and strolled over.

"Miss Care," he said, nodding his head in acknowledgment.

"Thanks for coming," Reece said. "I was going to be taking your statement this morning but something's come up that we need your help on. Come inside we can talk while I get updated on the crime scenes."

I followed Reece into the building with Brian insisting I go in front of him. Reece spoke to the desk sergeant who gave him two folders which he perused in silence. Then he led us into the sparsely furnished interview room.

"Audrey's kidnapped Miss Care's boss, where would she take him?" Reece said, talk about direct.

Brian nearly choked on his own breath. I clapped him on the back and he regained his composure. "Bloody hell that woman'll be the death of me," he said.

"Just so long as she's not the death of someone else," Reece said. I thought this a little heartless and glared at him. He ignored me.

"Well she might take him home or to the café but I expect you've checked there," Brian said.

"Men are there as we speak," Reece said, "I was thinking more obscure than that. Anywhere else?"

"She sometimes looks after an old ladies cat when she's away on holiday. I think she said she was going to Barbados for the winter. We could try there."

"We?" Reece said, "There won't be any we in this. I'll be going in with my officers, she's potentially dangerous."

"I don't think that's wise," Brian said in a sudden show of the man he might once have been, "you see," he hesitated and looked slightly abashed, "she worships me; in fact I'm beginning to think this might all be for me in a strange kind of way. All of the ladies taken I'd inadvertently mentioned to her and she gets kind of jealous. Well actually, very jealous. I think you'll need me there. I think I might be the only person that she'll listen to."

Reece shook his head,

"I don't like taking civilians it's too risky," he said.

"You've got Miss Care with you, and besides, I feel like this is all my fault. If I'd confronted being a parent earlier and given her the support she needed she might not have become so," he seemed to search for the right word, "agitated."

Mental was the word that had sprung to my mind but his would do.

"Right you can come with us as long as you only talk and don't try and storm the building or something daft, we're not in the army any more," Reece said.

"When were you in the army?" I said, momentarily distracted.

"Not now, Care," he said in a way that led me to believe he'd been a drill sergeant, but it did have the effect of shutting me up.

The lady whose cat Audrey looked after lived at the end of Audrey's avenue. It seemed to be the house that had given the road its name and in whose garden the subsequent properties were built. Not wanting to announce our presence before it was established whether she was there or not, we parked outside Audrey's neighbours and I noted the officer posted at her door. The curtains in the living room twitched ever so slightly and I surmised that Ian was inside. Brian had seen it too and raised his hand in acknowledgement. The curtain fell back into place immediately.

The driveway to Smithson House was long and neglected. The brambles had all but concealed the two lines of York stone that delineated the expected path of any visiting vehicle. I was transported to another age where a carriage would have made this journey and was only snapped out of my reverie by Brian calling out, "Miss Care mind out!" as my ankle descended into an uncovered drain. Luckily it just jolted me as it was a drain that took away surface water and not one to the mains. It brought me back to the present moment and reminded me that we could be in danger.

The tomboy part of me still thought I could whip Audrey in a girl on girl fight. Concentrate Care, this isn't a story it's real and Mr De'Ath could be in that house, drugged, tied up helpless. I smiled. No really it wasn't in the least funny.

Actually it wasn't.

The outside of the house was slightly better looked after than the driveway would suggest but it looked empty. The curtains were drawn in most of the rooms and a light had been left on in an upstairs bedroom perhaps to fool an observer that there was someone inside. We approached cautiously behind Reece when there was a sudden crack as a cat shot out of the cat flap in the back door. Managing not to exclaim only by shoving my hand over my mouth, I breathed deeply until my heart rate returned to normal.

Reece's hand reached for the back door handle and I half expected another shock. Nothing happened other than the door opening. He disappeared into the kitchen and I felt real fear.

"Clear!" he said in a somewhat FBI fashion.

We followed him into the room and looked about. The house looks like all houses do when their owners are away, neat, tidy and just a little bereft. Reece was already out into the hallway and motioned for us to remain quiet. We froze as a loud noise came from the floor above. It sounded like a chair scraping across the floor and it set my teeth on edge. It was followed by a loud thump and then silence.

"Stay here. I don't want you coming upstairs okay?" Reece said, "Get under the stairs and stay out of sight no matter what you hear. Understood?"

Brian and I nodded and took shelter in the cavernous under-stair space. I had never appreciated how difficult it is to hear something happening and interpret what it is. The next thing that we heard was a thump, a similar scraping sound to before and a voice shouting,

"No!"

The voice was definitely male but beyond that it was hard to tell. It was followed by footsteps descending the stairs and just as my curiosity got the better of me and I poked my head round the corner my world exploded in pain. Again.

TWENTY-EIGHT

I was flying across the sea it was a peaceful feeling but something was tugging at my arm. I shook it off. I didn't want to stop flying. "Let go! Get off!"

"Care, wake up. Care, please wake up. They're getting away."

"Don't care," I said.

"You will if I leave you here Care. Come on," Reece said hauling me none too delicately up by my arm and out into the car. He was gentler then and settled me into the front passenger seat and strapped me in.

"That's the second time you've been hurt in my vicinity. Perhaps staying with me wasn't the best idea."

"Mmmm it feels like the best idea," I said cuddling up to his arm.

"Let go Care, d'you want me to crash?" Reece said, taking the corner too fast and overcorrecting.

"Who're we following anyway?"

"Brian, Audrey grabbed him and took off."

"How'd she get past you to Brian?"

"She took the back stairs. I went up, she came down."
His tone precluded further interrogation.

Had I just caressed Reece's arm? Oh Lord, I've got to
stop getting knocked out, it was making me affectionate and
random and out of control. I hate being out of control.

"That's their car," Reece said speeding up.

It was a Blue estate and I could only see one person
the one driving. "Where's Brian?" I said.

"I suspect Brian is that peculiar shaped lump in the
back."

"What is it with this woman? She looks normal but
she's got the strength of two weightlifters," I said.

"It might be her mental state giving her extra strength.
Whatever it is, she must be desperate. They're turning off. I
don't think she's seen us."

"Isn't this the back of the Golf Club?" I said, "Near
Hole nine."

"Ahuh and I think I know where she's going. Are you
okay? Can you manage to stay with me?"

I touched my nose gingerly. It hurt but the hurt
actually brought clarity. "I'll be fine let's get them." We
parked about a hundred yards back and walked to the car.

"How'd she get Brian out so quickly? I mean he's not a small man."

"She's got help," Reece said as he pushed on through the undergrowth at the rear of the course.

"Who are we looking for?" I said still clueless.

He stopped suddenly and placed his finger across my lips. Even in my tense state the touch of his finger sent a jolt where it had no place to go. Get a grip Care. I could hear voices. One more familiar than the others.

"You wait until I get out of here. You've not heard the last of this. I have contacts," Mr D.

At least he was still alive.

"Shut up or she'll make sure you never get out of here," said a male voice, younger and strangely familiar.

"Ian," Reece said.

"But he rescued me," I said.

"Yes he's got a soft spot for you," Reece said. "We ought to wait for back-up really."

We were crouching in amongst nettles and brambles behind a shed that looked as if it was used to store items the golf club had forgotten they had. The windows were covered in something green. Reece crept nearer very stealthily but you couldn't see much. He came back.

"We'll not risk it unless we have to........."

"AAAAArrgh!"

We both stood up. It was difficult to tell who had yelled.

"AAAAArrgh!"

A dark shape was headed directly for the window nearest to us and it just kept coming and coming. Reece pushed me to one side straight into a particularly nasty patch of nettles then what I can only describe as a giant roll of carpet launched through the window and landed where we had just been standing.

The roll of carpet was struggling left to right, right to left. Reece loosened the rope tying it in place and a very angry Brian emerged from the centre.

"Where's that ruddy woman?" Brian said turning round and looking back through the hole in the window he'd just made.

Surveying the wreckage we were able to gather that Brian had managed to bowl over Ian who was lying unconscious under a pile of golfing trollies. Audrey and Mr De'Ath were nowhere to be seen.

"I'm going to kill her," Brian shouted and made to run after them both but his feet were still tied together and he fell flat on his face.

"No you're not," Reece said, as back up finally arrived. "Officer keep Mr Weatherall here, do not let him out of your sight. There's another man under that pile of golf trollies, if he's not too badly injured handcuff him and keep him here until I get back. Care you're with me. You two, with us let's go. There's a woman ahead who's dangerous and she has a hostage. No sudden moves."

The path through the undergrowth became less dense as we approached the ninth hole but there was no sign of Audrey and Mr D.

"Let's split up. You two over there; Care come with me this way."

We ran twenty metres and came across a man lying on the ground waving a putter in the air, "Woman! Woman! That way," he wheezed pointing in the direction of the clubhouse. We set off in pursuit. Reece and the other officer were clearly fit but I was already puffing and my legs were beginning to cramp. It was only my stubbornness that kept me going, that and the thought that if Mr D. died I'd have to put up with Reg for good. I didn't know before today just how big golf courses were, I always thought they were just like large putting greens. They are if a putting green is the size of Lake Windermere.

We left the rough on hole number one and saw a shock of blonde hair racing into the club room. Back to where it all began.

"Why would she go in there?" Reece said. "It's so public."

"P'raps she doesn't care anymore Gov," one of the officers, who'd caught us up, said.

I tried to speak but nothing would come out. I felt like my lungs would never work again. Reece and the other officer moved to the doors keeping out of sight. I literally crawled to a spot just behind them.

"I've got a knife to his throat. I'll kill him I tell you!" said a shrill female voice.

TWENTY-NINE

I'd've paid good money to see the look that appeared on Oswin Smarmer's face with Audrey's proclamation, but I was too worried about Mr De'Ath to appreciate it fully.

The boss was looking every inch of his name. Audrey's mania must have delivered the strength needed to drag him across the golf course, even his knees were covered in grass stains and his colour was light charcoal. His eyes were flitting about the room as if he wasn't quite sure where he was and, given her previous use of mind numbing drugs, I wouldn't have put it past her to have used something on him. She saw us entering and pressed the steel blade closer.

Whenever I'd thought about being in a situation where there was potential violence I'd always thought that I'd be scared and runaway. I mean I can't even watch violence on the television. It therefore surprised me at how icy calm and just downright angry I was. How dare this woman behave like this. It didn't matter what she'd been through, she couldn't just go round drugging people and holding knives to their throat. I began to take a step forward but a strong well shaped arm held me back.

"No Care let me handle this," Reece said his look understanding but commanding; "I don't want to have to arrest you for interfering with police business."

I nodded but kept close behind him.

"Audrey why don't you let him go, it's me you want to hurt. It's me that hurt you, darling. I'm sorry," Brian said softly from behind me.

Reece tensed but let him speak.

"I'm sorry I wasn't there for you and Ian. Please let him go, he's not well. Take me. I'll come with you wherever you want to go," Brian said taking a step forward. She seemed to consider it for a moment but then the knife returned to its former position.

"Nice try Brian but it's not your fault, it's his," Audrey said pulling on Mr De'Ath's arm. "If he hadn't run that announcement none of this would have happened."

Okay she'd officially lost me now. Announcement?

"That's what this is all about?" Brian said inching forward again.

Reece moved forward with him keeping quiet taking it all in.

"You know it is, don't pretend it made no difference. I know it did. All your fancy friends laughed and you couldn't stand it, could you, being shown up like that to the tennis bunnies." Audrey made her contempt of them clear as she spat on the floor after the last two words.

Over her shoulder I could just make out a person's hand tentatively reaching for her arm. She hadn't noticed.

"I heard them laughing at me with their snooty voices, 'Have you seen her hair? And her nails what a fright!' I showed them didn't I? I should have killed 'em while I had the chance, while they were helpless instead of propping them up but I wanted him to know why I done it. He pretended he didn't know nothing about it. Can you believe it?"

"Actually…" I said but a further commanding look silenced me.

As I spoke she turned towards me and Oswin took his opportunity and grabbed her arm, pulling the knife away from Mr De'Ath's throat. The knife went skimming across the maroon pile behind a curtain. At the same time Brian came flying past my head, launching himself at Audrey who emitted a faint squeal and disappeared under a tweed clad body.

Oswin pulled Mr D. behind the bar to safety.

Reece leapt forward and separated Brian and Audrey just as another P.C. brought in a handcuffed Ian.

"Mum!" Ian shouted and wrenched himself away to kneel by his clearly wounded mother.

Brian was looking at his blood soaked hands in a daze. Reece was already applying pressure to the wound.

"Care ambulance now!" he shouted. I was already dialling.

"Mum don't leave me Mum!" Ian said weeping into his mother's hair.

I could see the wound was in the middle of her body somewhere. Biology not having been my strongest subject at school I didn't know if the wound was serious enough to cause death but the middle didn't seem a good place to be stabbed. The ambulance was taking an age and Audrey was turning a most peculiar colour.

"Brian," was all she could say and Ian's face was overcome by the deepest anguish as he realised his mother's dying words were not for him, the loyal son, but for the philanderer who had consumed her every waking moment since he had carelessly seduced her and cast her aside in his youth.

Our eyes met and seeing in them the pity that I couldn't conceal he hung his head and his tears dropped onto the platinum tresses below.

THIRTY

"Is she going to be okay?" I asked as Audrey was bundled into the ambulance.

"I don't know," Reece said, "how about you?"

"Oh me, I'm always okay," I said. He raised his eyebrows, took Ian's arm and led him to the car. I surveyed the bar and my grey eyes met the piercing blue of Oswin Smarmer.

"Quite the hero," I offered.

"Quite the shiner," he countered.

I looked at myself in the mirror and concurred. He'd actually been quite polite. My face was a mess. It was only because there was limited space in the ambulance and the fact that I was walking that meant that I hadn't earned a place in the hospital wagon. The adrenaline was beginning to wear off and as the shock of what had just happened began to sink in, I literally sank to the floor. My legs felt like they had no bones in them.

The doors of the club room burst open and both Felicity and Donna flew into the room. They pulled me to my feet, sat me on a velour bench and began ordering various liquors and making sure I drank them.

"Darling girl you were so brave," Felicity said brushing my clothing in a vain attempt to undo the damage.

"Oswin phoned us and told us what you'd been through and we just had to come. Us girls must stick together," Donna said through a waft of very expensive perfume.

I balked slightly at the description of either them or me as girls but then, softened by the drink and the comfort of being fussed over, sank back into the velvet softness of plush upholstery and relaxed.

It turned out the drinks were on the house and we all had a very jolly time telling and re-telling the tale of the day's events. However I couldn't shake the melancholia entirely and eventually called a taxi to take me home. Reece texted that Audrey was stable and Ian was talking which relieved my mood a little before I sank gratefully into my bed and slept the sleep of the exhausted.

Something was banging. I sat up. Apart from the inside of my head, a noise was definitely coming from outside.

I checked that I had some clothes on (fully dressed though somewhat crumpled) and dragged my weary bones downstairs on my bottom, because this seemed to be the easiest way. I opened the door to see Reece looking clean and, let's face it, utterly gorgeous before me. He pushed passed me into the kitchen.

"Care how are you this morning? Hangover?"

I attempted speech and a kind of grunt emitted from my lips.

"You know the best cure for a hangover. Strong coffee and a sausage and egg muffin."

He held up a familiar red and yellow bag and wafted it under my nose. My stomach gave a large growl and I grabbed it from him and ate it without so much as taking a breath. He chuckled and filled the kettle.

"Glad to see your appetite is undiminished," he said. "Coffee?"

"Mmm..Mmm," I managed.

He sat opposite me and leaned his elbows on the table. "Audrey's going to be okay," he said, "she won't be out in public for a long while but she'll live. Brian's paying for her lawyer and Mr De'Ath has been discharged from hospital properly this time."

I had a feeling Mrs D. would spoil him for a while and I smiled.

Reece continued "The announcement was Audrey's engagement to Brian, turns out he sent it in to the paper in a moment of weakness but changed his mind and asked Mr De'Ath to pull it. He forgot and Brian folded under the pressure of his peers and ended it."

"What was the nail varnish all about?" I said, suddenly remembering the poisonous coloured bottles.

"She overheard the bunnies, as she calls them, taking the mickey out of her fuchsia talons and decided to leave a bottle in each room so that Brian would be sure to see it and believe that their taste was no better than hers. Nail polish inverted snobbery if you like," Reece said as he finished making his cup of coffee.

"What will happen to Brian?" I said.

"I doubt he'll be charged with anything. He tried to stop her hurting anyone else and the knife was caught between them, I can't see a jury convicting."

"And Ian?" I said after finishing my last mouthful.

"He helped her all the way through. He has a birth mark on his upper left arm shaped like Australia. He's also going away for a long time."

I must have looked sad because he said,

"He helped drug you and three others, kidnapped you and didn't care if you lived or died."

"I know but you should have seen his face when all his mother could do was call out for Brian. It nearly broke my heart," I said.

Reece got up from his chair knelt down beside me and held my hand in his much larger one. "Care has anyone ever told you, you're a big softy" he said massaging the back of my hand.

"Me, Care the tomboy. Never," I said as I smiled.

His hand moved up to my cheek and I held my breath.

"Now Care about this charge of attempting to interfere with a police officer in the line of his duty. I was wondering do you want to take it any further?" Reece said as his lips moved towards mine.

"Oh I do, I so do," I said in my last coherent thought for some time.

THE END